TRIPLET TROUBLE
and
the Bicycle Race

There are more books about
the Tucker Triplets!

TRIPLET TROUBLE
and
the Bicycle Race

by Debbie Dadey and Marcia Thornton Jones
Illustrated by John Speirs

A
LITTLE APPLE
PAPERBACK

SCHOLASTIC INC.
New York Toronto London Auckland Sydney

To the original Helen — Helen Perelman.
Thanks for being a real pro at fixing
things!

— MTJ and DD

ISBN 0-590-90731-X

12 11 10 9 8 7 6 5 4 3 2 1   7 8 9/9 0 1 2/0

Printed in the U.S.A.   40

First Scholastic printing, April 1997

Contents

1

The Race Is On

"Who likes to play computer games?" Mr. Parker asked our second-grade class. Everyone raised their hands. Even me. My name is Sam Johnson.

Alex Tucker stood up and shouted, "Me!"

Mr. Parker didn't say anything. He just looked at Alex and cleared his throat. In a minute, Alex sat down. Alex is a good friend of mine, but sometimes she forgets to raise her hand.

"Our school needs more computers. And we can all help," Mr. Parker said with a big smile.

Alex slumped down in her seat. "Oh, no," she moaned. "Are we going to have to sell candy?"

Ashley Tucker shook her head at her sister, Alex. "Don't be rude," Ashley said. "More computers for the school is a good thing."

"Computers are a good thing," Mr. Parker agreed.

Ashley smiled at Alex. Ashley always likes to give the perfect answer.

"But we don't have to sell candy to help buy computers," Mr. Parker said.

Alex stuck out her tongue, then grinned at Ashley.

Adam Tucker raised his hand. Adam, Ashley, and Alex are triplets, the Tucker Triplets. They look alike, but they definitely don't think the same.

Adam is very smart. He asked a smart question. "If we aren't going to sell candy," he asked, "then how are we going to raise money?"

Mr. Parker took a piece of red chalk and wrote BICYCLE RACE in big letters. "We are going to race for computers," he said with a smile. "We'll get pledges for money to finish the race."

"All right!" the class cheered. Barbara and Randy clapped. Maria was so happy she waved her hands in the air.

"I love to ride my bicycle," Barbara said.

"I just got a new bike for my birthday," I said. I couldn't wait to ride it in the race.

"I bet I'll be the only racer in a wheelchair," Randy bragged.

"I bet I win," Adam told the class.

"No, you won't," Alex said. "I'm going to win."

"No, I will win the race," Ashley bragged.

I knew what that meant. The triplets were going to try to beat each other. And that meant trouble. Triplet trouble.

2

Practice Makes Perfect

"There's only one way to win," Randy said after school. "And that is to practice. Who wants to practice with me?"

"I would," Adam told him, "but I have to take this book back to the library."

"Sam and I are going to play ball," Alex said. "You can play with us."

Randy shook his head. "I think I should practice."

"I'll practice with you," Ashley said softly. "Come on, I'll race you to my house. I have to get my bike."

Randy rolled away in his wheelchair with Ashley running beside him.

"I don't need to practice anyway," Adam said, puffing out his chest. "I'm fast enough."

"Not as fast as me," Alex reminded him.

I looked at Randy and Ashley as they turned the corner. I didn't think that I needed to practice. My new bike was

extra fast and had five speeds. I didn't want to brag, but I was going to win the race.

"Come on," Alex yelled. "Let's play ball!"

I ran to play with Alex. In a few minutes, Ashley zoomed by on her bicycle.

Ashley had on a pink helmet with purple stripes. Randy zipped right beside her in his wheelchair. Randy had on a green helmet with stars on the side. They were really moving fast.

"Kick the ball," Alex shouted at me. I knew Alex wanted to win the race. So did Adam, Ashley, and Randy. But I had the newest bike. I was going to win!

3

Who Cares?

The next day was Saturday. I got up and polished my new bike. The chrome really shined! I rode over to the Tuckers' house to show the triplets.

Alex and Adam were already in their driveway. They were riding their bikes in circles.

The triplets have old bikes. Alex's bike

12

is the worst. It's covered with scratches and dents.

My dog, Cleo, barked and ran in circles after them. Alex laughed when Cleo got so dizzy she panted and plopped in the grass.

Adam zipped around me on his bike. "I'll race you, Sam," he said. "I'm faster than everybody!" he yelled.

Alex yelled back, "You're not faster than me!"

I didn't say anything. I knew that I had the fastest bicycle.

"I can prove it right now," Adam told her. "I'll race you to the corner."

But just then the garage door opened. There sat Ashley on her pink bike. She had on a matching pink shirt and shorts. But nobody was looking at them. We were looking at her helmet.

Ashley had stuck stickers all over her helmet. When she rode her bike onto the driveway, the sun made the stickers sparkle. She rode her bike extra slow.

We could all see her decorated helmet.

I always liked the black thunderbolts on my helmet. But Ashley's sparkling stickers looked better than thunderbolts.

"Who cares about a helmet?" Adam told her.

"Adam is right," I said. But I really liked Ashley's stickers.

We all looked at Alex. She was very quiet. Alex didn't answer, but her eyes were big. That could only mean one thing. Alex was thinking up another one of her brilliant ideas.

4

Alex's Surprise

Alex snapped her fingers right in front of her nose. I couldn't wait to hear her brilliant idea. Alex didn't tell me. She didn't tell anybody. She just took off her helmet.

Alex's helmet used to be shiny purple. That's when it was new. Now it's full of scratches.

Alex looked at her helmet. Then she looked at Ashley's. Ashley smiled and turned her head so the sun shone on her stickers.

Alex let her bike fall in the grass next to Cleo. Then she stomped into the garage. I ran after her.

"Aren't you going to practice?" I asked Alex.

Alex shook her head. "There isn't time," Alex said. "I have to decorate my helmet."

"But it doesn't matter if Ashley's helmet looks better than yours," I said. I shouldn't have said Ashley's helmet was better. Alex hates when her sister and brother do things better than she does.

Alex stuck out her chin and stomped her foot. "Mine will be better. Just wait and see."

Alex took a bottle of glue and ran out to the backyard. Adam and Ashley didn't see her. They were too busy zooming down the sidewalk. Ashley was in front, but Adam was close behind. I didn't wait to see who won. I wanted to see what Alex was doing.

I found her in the backyard. Her helmet was on the ground. She was picking dandelions and putting them inside her helmet. I got down on the ground and helped her. Cleo bounded into the backyard, too. Cleo didn't help. She tried to eat the dandelions. Alex and I picked dandelions until her helmet overflowed with bright yellow flowers.

Then Alex went back inside the garage. I started to follow her, but she turned and pointed a finger at my nose.

"You have to stay outside," she said. "This is a surprise."

I sat down next to Cleo and waited. I scratched Cleo's ears. Cleo was glad it took Alex a long time.

Adam and Ashley rode up and stopped in front of me. They were out of breath from riding so fast.

"Aren't you going to practice?" Ashley asked.

"I want to see what Alex is doing," I said. "Then I'll practice."

Adam and Ashley parked their bikes. We all sat together to wait for Alex.

Finally, Alex came out of the garage.

Alex looked like she had sprouted a garden on her head. Yellow dandelions stuck out everywhere.

Ashley giggled. "You look like a walking flower."

Adam laughed out loud. "It's the silliest thing I ever saw."

"No, it's not," Alex said. Then she looked at me. "Tell them, Sam. My helmet is better than Ashley's, isn't it?"

I like the Tucker Triplets. They're my best friends. But when they put me in the middle, there's always trouble. I thought hard before I said anything. Then I looked at Alex. She smiled and turned her head so I could see her helmet. I could tell she thought her helmet was beautiful.

I knew there was one thing Alex liked. She liked to be different. I knew just what to say. "I've never seen anything like it." It was the truth.

Alex smiled so big I saw the space where her tooth used to be. Then she shook her head so hard two dandelions fell off her helmet. They floated down and landed on Cleo's head.

"I have a secret," she said.

"What?" Ashley asked.

Alex pressed her lips together and wouldn't say a word.

Ashley hates to be left out of secrets. "Tell us," she whined.

Adam jumped on his bike before she could answer. "Whatever Alex's secret is, it can't be more important than practicing. Let's go."

Ashley followed Adam. I didn't. I didn't know what Alex planned. But I knew one thing, Alex's plan was bound to be interesting.

5

The Worst Thing Ever

"What is your secret?" I asked. I looked at my shiny new bike. I wanted to ride it, but I wanted to know what Alex had planned even more.

Alex said, "Winning Mr. Parker's race isn't the most important thing."

I stared at Alex. "But you always like to win," I said.

Alex nodded. "Everybody likes to win. But this is a different kind of race. Winning only counts if we have pledges from lots of people agreeing to pay money for every lap we ride. That's how Mr. Parker will earn money for new computers. We have to get people to make pledges for the race."

Alex was right. If we didn't have any pledges, it wouldn't matter who won.

"How can we get pledges?" I asked.

Alex already had a plan. "We'll call all of our aunts and uncles and grandparents that send us birthday cards. Then we'll be the winners because we'll get the most pledges."

I rode my bike home and found the telephone book where my dad keeps important numbers. There weren't very many names. I was still hunting through the book when Dad came in from mowing the lawn. I told him what I was doing.

Dad took the pledge paper Mr. Parker gave us. He signed it three times.

I smiled. Sometimes I wish that I had a big family like the Tuckers. But I knew one thing. I had the best dad in the world.

The next day Alex held up a long list of pledges.

"No fair!" Adam yelled.

"You cheated!" Ashley hollered.

Alex folded her arms across her chest and stuck out her chin. "You're just mad because I thought about it first," she told Adam and Ashley.

"But who are we going to get to pledge?" Adam asked. "The bicycle race is just one day away."

"You called everyone we know," Ashley said. "You didn't leave anyone for us."

"Since I have the most pledges, I'm going to win the race," Alex bragged. Then she climbed on her old bike. She put on her helmet. The dandelions didn't look bright yellow anymore. When she tightened her helmet's chin strap a few flowers came loose and floated to the ground. She pedaled her bike down the sidewalk. "I'm ready to practice racing, now. Look! No hands!"

I looked at Adam and Ashley. They were mad.

"That's nothing," Adam told her. Adam stood up and rode his bike without any hands. He can't stand it when Alex does something better than him.

Alex coasted past me. Her handlebars wobbled and her bike zigged and zagged. "Aren't you going to try?" she yelled to me.

I looked down at my shiny new bike. There wasn't a single scratch on it. I wanted to keep it that way.

Ashley shook her finger toward Adam and Alex. "You'd better be careful or you'll both end up in the hospital," she warned. Ashley likes to follow rules. She held onto her handlebars with both hands.

"You're just mad because we're better than you," Alex yelled to Ashley. She looked over her shoulder at Ashley to say it. That's why she didn't see Cleo in front of her.

"Watch out!" I screamed. I didn't want Cleo to be smashed.

Alex saw Cleo just in time and swerved. That's when it happened.

Alex and Adam landed on the driveway. Arms, legs, handlebars, and wheels were all mixed up. I grabbed a hand and pulled. It was Alex.

Adam stood up and looked at his scraped knee. "Why did you run into me?" he asked Alex.

Alex dusted off the seat of her pants. Most of her dandelions were scattered on the ground. "It's Cleo's fault," she said. Cleo whined and licked Alex's hand. Alex scratched Cleo's head. Alex couldn't stay mad at my dog. She liked Cleo almost as much as I did.

I helped Alex pick up her bike. That's when she saw it. It was horrible. It was the worst thing that could have happened.

6

Sam's Perfect Plan

Alex's tire was flatter than a rubber band.

"You can't win the race now," Adam said.

"Pledges aren't good," Ashley added, "unless you ride in the race."

"And you can't ride in the race with a flat tire," Adam told her.

Adam and Ashley rode their bikes down the sidewalk and around the corner.

I've known Alex since kindergarten and I've never seen her cry. Not even when she lost her tooth. But now Alex's eyes were watery and her bottom lip trembled. I had to do something or my best friend was going to cry.

"We'll get it fixed," I said in a hurry. "It'll be okay."

"A new tire costs money," Alex sniffed.

She was right. I knew I didn't have enough money to buy a new tire. Alex sniffed again and threw her helmet on the ground. When a dandelion fell off, she smashed it with her sneaker. "This is all your fault," she said, "because Cleo is your dog. And Cleo made me crash."

Then Alex stomped into her house.

I had a terrible feeling that I would lose my best friend unless I thought up something quick. I stared at Alex's bike. Cleo whined and I scratched her ear. "How can I fix Alex's bike?" I asked Cleo.

Cleo didn't answer. She sat down and thumped her tail on the ground.

I was still staring at Alex's bike when Ashley and Adam came back. They parked their bikes. I looked at them. And that's when it hit me. The perfect plan.

"You have to help me," I told them. "We have to fix Alex's bike or she'll be mad at me forever."

"So?" Ashley said like she didn't care.

"I hate it when Alex is mad. She won't play. She won't even talk," I told them.

"I've been trying to get her to stop talking to me for years," Adam said. "You should be glad."

"If we don't help her she'll never talk to any of us again," I said.

"Fine with me," Ashley said.

"Me, too," Adam blurted out.

"But she can't be in the race without her bike," I told them.

Ashley shrugged. "Then we can have her pledges," she said.

I put my hands on my hips. "That will make Alex even madder. And if she gets madder, she'll make our lives absolutely miserable," I said. "And Alex is very good at making our lives miserable."

Adam looked at Ashley and Ashley looked at Adam. They knew I was right.

They nodded. "Okay," Adam said. "What's your plan?"

We huddled on the grass. I told Adam and Ashley my plan. They looked at me like I was crazy.

"No way," Ashley said. "I told her to be careful and she wouldn't listen. It's her own fault she wrecked her bike."

"You have to do it," I told them. "It's our only hope!"

7

The Best Surprise

Adam and Ashley ran inside. I raced back to my house. My piggy bank was hidden behind my underwear. I shook out all the money. Two quarters, three dimes, a nickel, and two pennies rolled out. It didn't look like very much. I counted it twice. Eighty-seven cents. I hoped Adam and Ashley had more.

They were waiting for me on the front porch. "I have three nickels," Adam said.

"I have three whole quarters," Ashley bragged. "I can't believe I'm going to waste it on Alex."

We spread our coins on the top step. I was still counting when Adam figured it out. "One dollar and seventy-seven cents," he said.

"That's not even two dollars," Ashley said. "It won't be enough."

"It has to be," I said. Adam and I grabbed the handlebars. Ashley took the back tire. Together, we carried Alex's bike down three streets, across the park, and all the way to the bicycle shop.

"Is it enough?" I asked Helen. She's the owner of the shop.

Helen looked at the coins in my hand. She shook her head. "Sorry, that won't do."

"But it's all we have," Ashley said.

"Alex will never forgive me if we don't get it fixed," I said sadly. "I'll lose my best friend."

Helen shook her head. "Money can't buy friendship," she said. "I know a better way."

"You mean you'll do it for free?" Adam asked.

"I won't do it," Helen said, "but you can." Helen showed us how to find the holes in Alex's tire by pouring water on the rubber. The air from the tire made bubbles in the water.

"Look!" I yelled. I pointed to a place where I saw tiny bubbles. "That's why her tire is flat."

Helen nodded. "Now, all you have to do is patch the holes." Helen showed us how to do that, too. The last thing we did was pump more air into the tire.

"Perfect!" Ashley cheered.

"But how much are the patches?" I asked.

Helen smiled. "They are exactly one dollar and seventy-seven cents!"

I gave Helen our money. We yelled thanks on our way out. We rolled Alex's bike all the way home.

"Alex is going to be so surprised," Adam said.

"But something is missing," I told them.

"What?" Ashley asked.

I snapped my fingers right in front of my nose, just like Alex would have done. "I know just the thing," I said. And then I told them my idea.

Ashley smiled. "It will be perfect," she said.

Adam nodded. "I can't wait until tomorrow," he said. "It will be the best surprise ever!"

8

And the Winner Is . . .

"Rolling, rolling, rolling," Ashley, Adam, and I sang as we pushed Alex's bike to her house. It was Monday morning. The day of the big race. Cleo wagged her tail as she followed us. Ashley giggled. "Your idea was perfect," she said.

Alex opened the door. There it was.

Her own bike. The tire was fixed. But best of all were the dandelions. They were tied to the spokes and the handlebars. I even tied dandelions to the fenders.

Ashley and Adam ran into the garage. They brought Alex her helmet. Bright new yellow dandelions covered it, too.

Alex grinned so big we could see the space where her tooth used to be. "You did this for me? Thanks!"

Alex looked at her bike. Then she looked at us. "You helped me, now I'll help you."

Alex pulled wrinkled papers out of her book bag. It was the list of people who pledged money for Alex and the bicycle race. Alex handed each of us a page.

"Now we all have plenty of pledges," she said.

"Thanks," I said. Adam and Ashley patted Alex on the back. I was glad we fixed the flat tire.

"Let's go race!" Adam said. We grabbed our bikes and rushed to school.

53

It was neat. The blacktop was set up like a racecourse. Everyone got a number to pin to their shirt. I got number four.

My dad cheered from the crowd of parents, "Go number four!"

I waved at him and got ready to race.

Mr. Parker held up a green flag.

"Remember," he said, "you are all winners. I'm proud of you all for helping the school."

Alex, Ashley, Adam, and I smiled at one another. Randy gave us a thumbs-up.

Then Mr. Parker shouted and dropped the flag. "On your mark. Get set. GO!"

We were off. I raced as fast as I could. On my new bike, I was fast, but so were Randy and Adam. Alex was keeping up with me on her old bike. Dandelions flew everywhere. Things were a blur at the finish line.

Did I win? My heart pounded. I beat Adam. I even beat Alex. Randy and I tied. But someone crossed the finish line ahead of me.

It was someone with sparkling stickers on her helmet. "Ashley!" I shouted. "You won the race!"

Ashley nodded. "I think it was the stickers that helped."

Alex shook her head. I was afraid Alex would be mad that Ashley won. But she wasn't. "It was the practice that helped you win," Alex said. "Three cheers for Ashley! Hurrah!"

Everyone clapped and cheered for Ashley.

Sure, I wanted to win. But, it's nice when your friends win, too. And it's the nicest of all when you have friends like the Tucker Triplets.

TRIPLET TROUBLE

Debbie Dadey and Marcia Thornton Jones

Triple your fun with these hilarious adventures!

Alex, Ashley, and Adam

mean well, but whenever they get involved
with something, it only means one thing —
trouble!

○ BBT90730-X	Triplet Trouble and the Class Trip	$3.50
○ BBT90728-X	Triplet Trouble and the Cookie Contest	$2.99
○ BBT58107-4	Triplet Trouble and the Field Day Disaster	$2.99
○ BBT90729-8	Triplet Trouble and the Pizza Party	$2.99
○ BBT58106-6	Triplet Trouble and the Red Heart Race	$2.99
○ BBT25473-1	Triplet Trouble and the Runaway Reindeer	$2.99
○ BBT25472-3	Triplet Trouble and the Talent Show Mess	$2.99

Send orders to:
Scholastic Inc., P.O. Box 7502, 2931 East McCarty Street, Jefferson City, MO 65102-7502

Please send me the books I have checked above. I am enclosing $_____(please add $2.00 to
cover shipping and handling). Send check or money order—no cash or C.O.D.s please.

Name_____ Birthdate __/__/__

Address_____

City_____ State _____Zip _____

Please allow four to six weeks for delivery. Offer good in the U.S.A. only. Sorry, mail orders are not available to residents
of Canada. Prices subject to change.

TT